CAT + GABBY:
Mermaid Mystery

VICKI D. TURNER

Author: Vicki D. Turner
Cat & Gabby: Mermaid Mystery

ISBN: 978-1-7374681-2-7

Printed and bound in the United States of America.

DEDICATION

THIS BOOK IS DEDICATED TO
CLARKE TURNER & GABRIELLE GATEWOOD. THESE ARE TWO OF THE
MOST INSPIRATIONAL LITTLE GIRLS I KNOW. MY HOPE IS THAT YOU
BOTH CONTINUE YOUR LOVE FOR READING AND YOUR VIVID
IMAGINATIONS. I PRAY THAT YOU ALWAYS DREAM IN COLOR.

1

She gasped. Her eyes grew big. This had to be some crazy dream, right? Cat rubbed her eyes as if hoping to activate some magical genie in a bottle. Peeking from behind her hands, she slowly allowed one eye to open. Nope! This wasn't a dream. All Cat had hoped for was a normal weekend with her cousin. Let's face it though! No weekend with Gabby was ever really normal...

Mom's voice pierced through the quilted comforter making its way to

Cat's ears. "Good morning my shining star."

"Good morning," she managed through her lengthy yawn. Cat pulled the covers back and blinked until her eyes began to focus.

It was Saturday or was it? It seemed like Cat had woken up before the sun did. As much as she looked forward to Gabby's visit, she looked forward to sleeping in a little bit more.

"Let's go ahead and get you ready so that we can get to the store before your Aunt and Gabby arrive," Mom said.

"Are we still going to the craft store?" Cat asked, sliding out of the bed.

"Of course, sweetie," Mom smiled. "That's why we need to hurry and get going."

Yes! This was music to her ears! Cat hopped up with a sudden burst of energy and excitement. She ran to her mom and wrapped both arms around her.

"You're the best mom ever," Cat exclaimed. "I'll be down in 10!"

Cat had always been a high achiever and enjoyed learning very much. Beyond that, she loved to explore her creativity! Where one student saw a piece of paper, Cat saw an opportunity for an artistic masterpiece. For her, beauty was everywhere and in everything. The world was her canvas and that's a part of what made her so special.

"It's been 12 minutes now!" Mom urged from downstairs.

"Coming, Mom!" Cat yelled from the top of the stairs. She skipped back to her room and grabbed her sketchbook off of her dresser. She had to stay prepared for any inspiration that she might see along the way.

Cat enjoyed quality time shopping with Mom, but shopping with Dad allowed for her to add a few extras in the basket. Dad always had a difficult time turning down her smiling eyes. He always reminded her that everything she picked out was because she deserved it. This go-round, Dad was away for a work retreat, so Cat would have to stick to *the list* instead.

The list. Mom always had a list that she had taken time and care to create. The list kept them on track and focused on what it was that they needed. Cat was in control of checking off the list as they strolled down each aisle. The new fabric kit for her dolls was 7th on the list, so all was well in Cat's world.

On the drive home, Cat pressed her head against the passenger window. The clouds were particularly beautiful that day. Cat reached in her bag for her sketchbook and flipped it open to a blank page. There were wispy clouds and puffy clouds. There were floating clouds and then clouds that seemed to sit still. Cat pressed the lead against the page as she drifted off into her drawing. She sketched with one continuous stroke that never seemed to cease. It was endless just like the sky that she was inspired by.

When they arrived home, Cat helped put the groceries away in the pantry while Mom got breakfast started. The smell of scrambled eggs and cinnamon french toast swirled around the kitchen.

"Gabby should be arriving soon," Mom began. "I know that I don't have to tell you this, but make sure you girls listen to Savannah while your Aunt and I are gone."

Not only was Dad away for work, but Cat's mom and Aunt were going to be gone to attend a wedding for a day. Cat and Gabby had always looked forward to time with their babysitter, Savannah. She was crafty, fun, and she cared for them as if they were her own! Savannah was more than a sitter. She was family.

"Of course, Mom!" Cat smiled. "We won't let you down!"

This would be the first time that Mom left Cat overnight and Cat wanted to make sure to ease her Mom's worries and make her proud. As Cat finished setting the table, the doorbell rang.

"I'll get it," Cat said hurrying to the door. She peeked through the window to see her Aunt and a smiling Gabby with fresh braids dangling over her shoulders. Cat swung the door open and greeted Gabby and her aunt.

"Race you upstairs," Gabby said, jetting past Cat and heading for the stairs.

"No, no, no running," Mom yelled. "I don't want you girls hurting yourselves."

"They'll be just fine," Gabby's mom reassured.

Gabby slowed her sprint to a speedy walk to Cat's room and tossed her bag onto the bed. Cat crossed her arms and shook her head from side to side.

"Gabby!" Cat shouted. "Your bag goes right here in the closet". Cat motioned for Gabby to move her bag to its proper place.

"That's no way to greet your favorite cousin," Gabby laughed as she grabbed her bag off of Cat's bed.

The girls took turns washing their hands before heading down for breakfast.

"Did I tell you that we got a new dog?" Gabby asked, turning towards Cat.

"Well, I guess I won't be visiting you anytime soon," Cat said, raising her brow.

All Gabby could do was smile. Cat never had liked animals too much, but Gabby would rescue them all if she could. Where Cat saw frightening creatures, Gabby saw friendly companions. Gabby was one of the toughest girls that Cat knew, but she had a tender concern for people and animals alike.

One time Gabby convinced Cat to help her build steps out of her dad's old crates so that she could rescue a kitten that was stuck in their oak tree.

Cat was a nervous wreck as she held down the base. One wrong step and Gabby could have gotten seriously hurt, yet Gabby was fearless like that. There was a silent admiration that Cat had for Gabby because of that.

The girls took bites out of their breakfast as Cat's mom went over the ground rules that they heard every time before Savannah came.

"No sweets before bed...clean up after yourselves...no food upstairs," Mom went on. Gabby's mom scrolled through her phone shaking her head as if she too had heard it all before.

"...and what time is bedtime?" Mom asked the girls.

"10!" Gabby shouted.

Cat glanced over at Gabby, "Bedtime is 9 PM, Mom."

"That's right, Cat," Mom said with a nod. "Nice try, Gabby."

Gabby shrugged and giggled as the girls walked their plates over to the sink to be rinsed off.

Savannah's car pulled into the driveway as Gabby's mom walked to the door to open it.

"Hey there, Savannah," Gabby's mom greeted. "Come right on in!"

"Thank you so much for being able to stay the night with the girls," Cat's mom added in from the kitchen.

"Of course!" Savannah smiled. "There's no two girls I would rather spend my time with."

Cat and Gabby sped over to Savannah and showered her with love and hugs!

"I can't wait to show you my new drawings," Cat said. "My teacher says I have the potential to win the district art show this year!"

"That's awesome," Savannah said, embracing Cat with another hug. "I wouldn't expect anything less from you!"

"And I scored 3 goals at our last home game last week," Gabby included. "My mom wants to invite you to the first tournament game!"

"Wow, you truly are the people's champ, Gabs," Savannah said raising her hand for a high five.

Gabby jumped up in excitement and clapped her hand with Savannah's. Cat and Gabby grabbed Savannah's bags and headed to the guest room. They could hear Cat's mom going over the list with Savannah as Gabby's mom interrupted to assure once again that everything would be alright! The girls looked at each other and exchanged chuckles.

"Got to love them," Gabby remarked.

"We really should be getting on the road now," Gabby's mom declared. "Savannah, you have our numbers and we'll call you as soon as we arrive at the wedding venue."

Savannah nodded as the girls entered the living room for their mothers' send-off. Cat and Gabby both gave their moms big hugs as they vowed to be on their best behavior once again.

"We love you girls," Cat's mom said. "We'll call and check-in soon and listen to Savannah…"

Gabby's mom nudged her sister out the door, closing it behind her.

"Alright! Race you upstairs," Gabby said dashing past Cat once again.

CHAPTER TWO

2

The day was perfect for spring. Pale pink skies faded into the white hues of the clouds. The slight breeze was surprisingly comforting. It served as a subtle hint that summer was close, yet hadn't quite arrived.

Although Cat had been up pretty early that day, the girls always made the most of their time together. Savannah was in the kitchen ordering pizza, while Cat and Gabby were in the backyard soaking in the last bit of sun.

"Look at me," Gabby yelled. "This thing goes really high."

Cat glanced up at Gabby as she pierced through the air going back and forth on the wooden swing.

She began to notice that each time Gabby flew forward, her braided strands suspended in the air just as long as she did. Even though each plait was individually woven, they all went up together and all fell down together. Before Cat knew it, she was weaving lines with her chalk on the pavement.

"Let's see how far I can jump," Gabby giggled.

"I don't think that's a good idea," Cat murmured, shaking her head because deep down she knew that at any moment Gabby would be launching herself from the swing either way.

Gabby felt like she was on top of the world up high in her own special place. She gazed beyond the trees scanning her surroundings.

She saw kids across the fence bouncing up and down on the trampoline. The springing sounds of their jump mat paired with the swishing of the wind created a sort of rhythmic beat in her ears. She looked further into the distance taking in all of the nature around her.

The setting sun finally came into focus so if Gabby was going to jump, it would be now or never. Gabby folded her legs in as she motioned backward as far as she could. Dropping back forward against the wind, she extended her legs. Waiting until she was slightly higher than the ground, she leaped off of the seat. Gabby hovered in the air for what seemed like forever before gracefully landing on the grass.

"I'd say that was a perfect 10," Gabby said, flashing her bright smile at Cat.

"More like a 9.5," Cat teased, smiling back.

Gabby and Cat were cousins, but it felt like they were more like sisters. Even though they were the same age, Gabby loved to take charge. In Gabby's world, she was the boss or better yet, the Queen of Everything! There were very few things that she feared, and heights were definitely not one of them.

Savannah peeked her head past the sliding back door and motioned for the girls to come inside. Cat swept her hands together allowing some of the chalk dust to fall from her fingertips.

"You girls go ahead and get washed up so that we can eat," Savannah said.

The girls headed upstairs to Cat's room as Savannah picked up the ringing phone. Gabby dug through her duffle bag while she waited for her turn at the sink.

"Did you finish that skirt design for your Sasha doll?" Gabby called from the room.

Cat had already finished making the floral blouse for her doll and had begun working on the skirt the last time that Gabby was over.

"Almost!" Cat said, turning to point at it laying on her dresser.

Gabby picked up the mini denim skirt. "Too bad it isn't my size," she laughed.

"Mine either," Cat joked back.

The girls faintly heard Savannah still chatting downstairs.

"Yes, I'm glad that you all made it safely...they are getting washed up for dinner as we speak," Savannah spoke.

"That's probably just my Mom calling to check in," Cat spoke as she washed the remaining pastel chalk off of her hands.

Gabby nodded as they finished up and headed back downstairs.

They could smell the scent of the buttery-crusted pizza from the staircase. Savannah placed the phone back on the hook as Cat and Gabby entered the kitchen.

"Can we help set the table, Savannah," Gabby asked, batting her slanted, brown eyes.

Gabby's eyes often smiled even when she didn't. At least, that's what Savannah had always told her. Those eyes always worked to her advantage especially when she was trying to get us out of trouble that most times she had gotten them into.

"Of course you can," Savannah said.

"Just sit back and relax," Cat beamed as she set the placemats on the table.

Gabby grabbed three plates from the cabinet and placed each of them on the table. Cat poured the fruit juice into the cups as Savannah passed out the pizza slices.

"I'd say that was great teamwork, girls," Savannah said as they sat down and joined hands.

Nights with Savannah and the girls were always the best! Pizza, nachos, or some of the girl's other favorite foods were always on the menu. She would even let the girls watch a little television while they ate each time pinking promising with the girls to keep it their little secret.

"Rodgers & Hammerstein's Cinderella is a must-see," Savannah said, oozing with excitement. "I heard my mom going on and on over the phone with Ms. Street saying how much of a classic it was," Gabby responded. "Whatever that means!"

"Well, you know what they say," Savannah insisted. "Moms are always right, right?"

The girls shrugged their shoulders and began to laugh at the sight of their synchronous motion. Gabby took a bite of her pizza as the melted cheese strings clanged to her lip.

"Mmm...mmmm...gooey, cheesy, deliciousness," Gabby rejoiced.

"Just like I like it," Cat finished off feeling satisfied.

Savannah snickered reaching for the remote. She powered on the TV just as the house phone began to ring once again. She stood up from the table and headed toward the phone.

"One second, girls," she began. "Let me take this call and then we'll start the movie!"

"Sounds good to me," Cat smiled.

"Me too," Gabby added.

The girls agreed to save Savannah some time and began to clear off the dinner table. Cat was carefully stacking up the plates when she felt a persistent tug on her arm.

"Do you see that?" Gabby asked, pointing to the television. Gabby grabbed the remote and turned the volume up a few notches.

"Reporting live from your nightly news---bystanders spot a majestic creature on the shore of the Atlantic...later confirming it was a mermaid..."

"Wow!," Cat smiled, "a real-life mermaid!"

"No, Cat! Look closer," Gabby pointed, walking closer to the screen. She waved for Cat to come over!

"She was sitting right there on the rock perched like an eagle," the onlooker said. "Except she wasn't an eagle and she surely lacked feathers...she was a mermaid with scales, and a tail and everything.

As we got closer she disappeared into the water, but before she did we were able to at least get a picture."

The picture was projected on the screen and then zoomed in on the beautiful being. There she sat... golden skin sparkling beneath the sun. The waves of the ocean failed in comparison to thesandy brown tresses overflowing from the crown of her head. Orange and bronze scales formed down to the tips of the tails that trailed behind her like streams of ribbon.

Gabby looked flustered, slowly glancing over her shoulder to Savannah holding the phone to her ear still. Gabby swiveled her head back to the TV and once again toward Savannah.

"Could this be real? Half-fish, half-goddess," Cat questioned. "Well, if it is real, I'd say that it's pretty cool!"

Gabby stared at Cat puzzled at how Cat could not see what she was seeing. The resemblance was too obvious to miss it!

"Earth to Cat," Gabby said, snapping her fingers. "Doesn't this mermaid look familiar to you?"

Cat looked back at the screen, tilted her head, and even tried squinting. "Is she supposed to look familiar to me?"

Gabby shook her head in disbelief. She placed her hands on Cat's shoulders and turned her around facing the kitchen. Gabby used her eyes to signal Cat to look in the direction of Savannah.

"Cat," Gabby whispered. "Our babysitter is a mermaid..."

CHAPTER TWO

3

"We've been through this already, Gabby," Cat insisted. "Savannah is not a mermaid!"

"But she is," Gabby argued, pacing back and forth in Cat's bedroom.

"Savannah has babysat us since we were 4," Cat said. "Don't you think that we would've noticed if she were a majestical ocean creature by now?"

"But...she is," Gabby replied, powering up her iPad.

"Can we ever just have a normal weekend," Cat sighed as she plopped down on her oversized bean bag chair.

Normal? Complex, adventurous, unexpected, daring, and most times strange, but never ever is it normal.

Cat reflected on her weekend with Gabby a few Christmases ago. Gabby was convinced that Santa Claus had eaten the tooth fairy after her tooth failed to get picked up from beneath her pillow. To this day, Gabby still hasn't forgiven him for the magical coins she missed out on.

"Look at this," Gabby said, zooming in on the iPad screen with her fingertips. The local news had already published the Mermaid Mystery article online.

"It says that the mermaid was spotted on the Atlantic Coast," Gabby continued.

"So what?" Cat questioned growing frustrated.

"Well, didn't your mom say that Savannah was flying in from her vacation in Florida," Gabby stated, rolling her neck. "Isn't Florida on the coast of the Atlantic?"

"That's just a coincidence," Cat replied softly, this time growing more curious.

"Or is it?" Gabby said, handing the iPad to Cat.

Cat grabbed the iPad to take a closer look. She examined the photo closely this time. *There were tons of women with long, wavy hair and bronze skin,* Cat thought to herself. Besides, Savannah and the girls shared everything with each other. Surely Savannah would have told them if she was a mysterious mermaid!

Just then, Cat's door pushed open.

"Hey girls," Savannah said, peeking her head into the room. "What happened to you girls picking out a movie for us?"

"Oh! Umm! Well...", Cat stuttered.

Never leave it to Cat to have the right words to say during moments of panic.

"You know what, Sav, suddenly we are just so exhausted," Gabby cut in.

"Yeah! Exhausted," Cat repeated nervously sliding the iPad behind her back.

"Must've been all of that fun in the sun," Gabby said, smiling coyly at Sav.

"Yep! All that sun," Cat echoed.

"No worries girls," Savannah smiled back. "There's always tomorrow!"

The girls nodded as they climbed into bed. Savannah tucked a few loose strands of her hair behind her ear before reaching for the light switch. Cat sat up instantly noticing the mocha colored mark on her right forearm.

"Everything okay, Cat," Savannah asked.

Gabby sat up glancing at Cat who hadn't yet blinked.

"Uhh, she's fine," Gabby said laughing. "It's this new Freeze Like A Zombie Challenge we've been playing lately!"

Savannah shook her head giggling to herself.

"You kids nowadays, "Sav said, "make sure to get some rest girls!"

Savannah closed the bedroom door as Cat slithered out of her bed. She grabbed the iPad from the bean bag chair and zoomed back in on the mermaid photo. There it was! The same brown mark on the forearm of the mermaid was the same mark that she had just seen on Savannah's. *Could it be?*

"It could be because it is," Gabby answered. Cat didn't notice that she was thinking out loud.

The girls looked at each other and nodded.

"Our babysitter is a mermaid," the girls exclaimed, jumping up and down on the floor.

"Shh!"Cat said, "she'll hear us".

This was the best day ever! How often do you find out that your babysitter is not only the coolest sitter ever, but also that she's a gorgeous mermaid?

Gabby imagined all the things they could do together. Every time Gabby and her mom would go to the pool, she would always place her legs together and move them up and down propelling herself through the water like a mermaid. Now, she could actually swim with one!

Cat had collected a ton of seashells over the years. Some were rough, some pointy, some spiraled and some were smooth! Cat wondered if Savannah would let her design an ocean-inspired top for her. She had some leftover fabric from her doll pieces that would be epic for Sav!

"I can't wait to tell Mom!" Cat said with excitement!

"We can't just tell our moms," Gabby replied, remembering that she was dealing with an amateur.

"Well, why not," Cat asked.

"First, we have to prove it."

Prove it?! The picture! The news article! The beauty mark! Was that not proof enough?!

"No, it's not enough," Gabby answered back.

Cat was doing it again! The whole thinking out loud thing. Her excitement about their discovery slowly started to dwindle at the thought of what all was involved in "proving it".

Gabby picked up the iPad as Cat cringed at the sound of her tapping and swiping the screen like some mad scientist.

"Ah-ha," Gabby said, lighting up like a lamp. "I saw this mermaid episode one time on The Magic School Bus!"

Cat couldn't believe what she was hearing. Gabby couldn't be serious but she was.

"...or maybe it was Sid The Science Kid," Gabby went on. "Either way, I was able to locate the ingredients to the special mermaid potion online".

MAGIC MERMAID POTION
3 oz of water
1 tbsp of sea salt
3 flower petals
1 orange peel

"Wait!" Cat said, "it says the potion can only be drunk at night."

"Well, it looks like we should get started now shall we," Gabby smirked tip-toeing to the bedroom door. "You know the deal, Cat! You go downstairs and distract Savannah while I grab the ingredients…"

Gabby turned over her shoulder to see Cat with arms folded standing still as a statue.

"What if I don't do it," Cat questioned.

"Come on, Cat," Gabby pleaded. "Trust me! We won't get caught. Besides, don't you want to know if Sav is really a mermaid?"

Cat tapped her foot and sighed deeply. "Fine, but if we get caught it's all your fault!"

"Yeah yeah yeah," Gabby said as the girls slowly crept outside the door.

Gabby had gotten it wrong a few times before, but this time she had never been so certain! This was a Mermaid Mystery she was determined to unlock!

CHAPTER FOUR

4

"Impossible, for a plain yellow pumpkin to become a golden carriage. Impossible for a plain country pumpkin and a prince to join in marriage," Savannah sang along in perfect harmony.

Gabby gasped. "I can't believe it!"

"Can't believe what," Cat whispered, creeping slowly down the stairs.

"Sav's watching Cinderella without us," Gabby pouted.

"You have to be kidding me, Gabby!"

"You're right," Gabby sighed. "Let's focus on this mission first and we can tackle that mission later!"

Cat shook her head as she felt the moisture increase within the palms of her hands. Suddenly, she didn't feel too well. Her stomach was as woven as Gabby's braids. She could turn back now and make a run for it, but Cat knew that she wouldn't get too far up the stairs before Gabby would be tugging her back down.

Gabby turned back and faced Cat placing both of her hands firmly on her shoulders.

"Ok, Cat...I need you to distract Savannah," Gabby mumbled.

"No, no, and no," Cat said, walking back up the steps. "You said that you needed me to be the lookout, not the distractor."

"Well, would you prefer to slither and crawl past the dangerous jungle that is your living room to capture the ingredients from the refrigerator tomb instead," Gabby said, tapping her foot gently.

"Absolutely not!," Cat scowled. "This is silly! I'm going back upstairs."

"Cat, is that you?" Savannah called out, pausing the television.

The color from Cat's face left, returned, and then fled again!

"Umm..." Cat's voice shook as stepped forward down the stairs. She turned to look at Gabby who was grinning harder than the Cheetos cat.

"You got this," Gabby mouthed with two winks of an eye.

Cat wasn't buying it, but at this point, it was too late. She took a huge breath and drifted into the living room toward the couch.

"Hey, you! What happened to you going to bed, little one," Savannah asked.

"Well...it's just...I couldn't fall asleep," Cat replied, joining Savannah on the couch.

"Missing your parents aren't you?"

Bingo! Savannah was making this easy. Cat did miss her mom tremendously, so technically this wouldn't be a fib at all, would it?

"I miss them so much," Cat sighed. "I'm not used to both mom and dad not being here to tuck me in and tell me bedtime stories."

"Well, I'm sure that I can't beat your parents' wonderful storytelling, but I have been told that I'm pretty great at creating stories from the top of my head," Savannah smirked.

"I'll take that," Cat smiled, laying her head on Savannah's arm.

Gabby rose on her tippiest of toes and grabbed the spice jar of sea salt from the cabinet shelf. She measured 1 teaspoon and added it to the Mermaid mixture. She carefully pulled the drawer opeb making syre to avoid any creaking.

She grabbed a spoon and began to stir together the ingredients as the flower petals swirled around the bowl. If Gabby pulled this off, she'd go down in history as a Mystery Master for sure!

"That was a great story", Cat giggled. "Especially the part about the stripeless zebra! How about another one?"

"Alright...one more story and then it's off to bed."

"Oh my!" Cat's jaw dropped at the sight of Gabby on the floor on all fours.

"What's wrong?" Savannah questioned.

Gabby peaked her head from behind the couch as she crawled to the end table. She pressed her finger against her lips hoping that Cat wouldn't ruin it.

"Uh! How about a funny story this time" Cat said nervously. "I sure could use the laugh".

"Ah-ha! One certified comedy coming right up," Sav exclaimed.

Gabby sighed in relief. That was close! Proving their babysitter was a mermaid though was even closer! Savannah's drinking cup was in arm's reach. Here goes nothing...

Slowly, she slid the bottle from her back pocket. Shaking the potion carefully, Gabby watched the bubbles ooze and fizz to the rim. Savannah was getting to the good part of her story and Cat was doing a magnificent job braving the task of staying engaged and most importantly, in character.

Gabby swiftly tipped the potion over into Savannah's cup and then placed the empty bottle back into her pocket. Go Gabby! Go Gabby! Go! Mission accomplished!

Cat glanced over the sofa to see Gabby squirming toward the stairs.

"Ha! That's hilarious," Cat said, tossing her head back. It was an added effect that she had picked up from Gabby years ago. She began to think that she was a natural at this whole accomplice gig!

"Ha! That's hilarious," Cat said, tossing her head back. It was an added effect that she had picked up from Gabby years ago. She began to think that she was a natural at this whole accomplice gig!

Creak! Gabby's heart dropped as she placed her foot on the second step.

"Gabby, is that you?" Savannah called out.

Gabby turned around and stepped off of the stairs rubbing her eyes in a semicircular motion.

Cat was as still as a mannequin in a department store window. *Oh no! She's onto us! Why did I let Gabby talk me into this anyway?*

"Sav, I can explain," Cat exclaimed. "We were watching the new—"

"How thoughtful of you," Sav smiled. "We just finished some story time and now both of you girls should really be getting back to bed."

Cat shot up off the couch and scurried towards the staircase before Savannah could even finish saying goodnight. Gabby flung her arms around Savannah and hugged her tightly. She turned to walk toward the stairs before remembering the Mermaid Mystery potion.

"Did you want me to take your cup to the sink," Gabby asked.

Savannah reached for the cup and began sipping until it was empty. She nodded and handed the cup to Gabby to put away.

"Thanks, sweetie. You are always So helpful," Savannah observed.

Gabby headed to the kitchen and placed the cup in the kitchen sink. *Achoo*! Gabby peaked around the sliding kitchen doors. *Achoo!* Savannah sneezed again! *Was it working? Was it really working?*

Gabby strode to the stairs and waited for what seemed like forever.

She watched from around the corner of the steps. Our babysitter is a mermaid! This has to work!

CHAPTER FIVE

5

"I waited and waited and waited," Gabby stated in disbelief. "I waited so long that Sav eventually went to bed. Nothing changed. Nothing even happened."

Gabby buried her face into the pillow in disappointment. She just couldn't figure out what had gone wrong. She was sure to measure every petal and peel and every grain of salt and ounce of water precisely just as the potion called for. Nothing even happened.

"Maybe Sav just isn't the mermaid we thought she was," Cat added delicately, fluffing her pillow.

"Sav was the mermaid on the news! I just know she was".

"Ok, well maybe we should get some rest and just revisit everything at a later time," Cat suggested.

She sank underneath the covers and glanced over at Gabby. She looked so defeated. They had tried, and that's all anyone could ever do is try. Although, it just wasn't that simple for Gabby!

If there was ever a problem, Gabby would be there to solve it. If there was ever anything broken, Gabby would be right there to fix it. That was just who she was! She didn't try. She did. She never stopped until she did…

"Gabby, it's going to be okay," Cat assured. "There will be other days, other mermaids. Just get some sleep, alright?"

"Sure thing," Gabby mumbled back.

Sleep? How could she! Gabby tossed and turned all night. At one point she tried counting sheep. She counted

300. She was still wide awake!

Gabby tossed the covers back and looked over at her cousin who was sound asleep. She slowly slid out of the bed until she felt the carpet fibers in between her toes. Gabby was determined to figure out what went wrong. She wouldn't stop until she did.

Gabby made it downstairs to the kitchen and proceeded to lay out all of her ingredients once again. First, she measured 3 ounces of water into the cup. She dropped 3 flower petals into the water followed by 1 orange peel. As she began to measure the sea salt she realized something.

"Tablespoon?" Gabby thought aloud. "Tablespoon! I thought it was a tea-spoon earlier. No wonder it didn't work on Sav!"

Go Gabby! Go Gabby! Go! She was back in business! Now all she had to do was get Savannah to drink the potion again in the morning. Piece of cake. She had her favorite accomplice getting her beauty rest upstairs. She'd find a way to convince Cat to accept the job.

The potion began to fizz this time smelling a little sweeter. The scent swarmed and lingered in the air like fresh baked cookies making their way out of the oven. Gabby picked up the cup and brought it closer to her lips. Not only was Gabby the Mystery Master, but she was the ultimate taste tester too.

"Mmmm. This is delicious," Gabby said, pinching her thumb and fingers together. "This deserves a chef's kiss for sure!"

Gabby steadily pulled open the refrigerator and placed the remaining potion in the back behind the milk.

"Tomorrow is going to be perfect," Gabby smiled, quietly shuffling up the stairs. The girls would get to spend the day with their babysitter, the mermaid.

"Cat will have me to thank for that," Gabby whispered to herself as she climbed back into the bed.

At that moment, she must've counted nine sheep before joining Cat in a blissful sleep.

CHAPTER SIX

6

The striking rays of sunlight passed through Cat's draped curtains. The fascinating thing about the sun was that it never had to ask permission to shine so brightly. It just did! It's like it knew its purpose which was to spread its light to the world. Just like with Cat and Gabby! Regardless of their unique differences, when together they lit up each other's world every single time.

"Rise and shine girls!" Sav said in

rhythm with the taps she made on the bedroom door. "This is not a drill! Breakfast is ready."

Sav's footsteps grew quiet and faint as she headed down the stairs.

"Love at first scent," Gabby exclaimed sitting up in bed. "Smells like bacon!"

Cat uttered something that only cavemen would probably understand. Gabby shrugged and slipped out of bed.

"Ahhh!" Gabby yelled as she dropped to the floor landing on her fee... fin?!

"Gabby, do you have to be so..." Cat screamed. "Ahhhhhh!!" She jumped back against her headboard!

She gasped. Her eyes grew big. This had to be some crazy dream, right? Cat rubbed her eyes as if hoping to activate some magical genie in a bottle. Peeking from behind her hands, she slowly allowed one eye to open. Nope! This wasn't a dream.

"Gabby! What kind of joke are you

playing right now? Where... are... your...legs!!!!!"

For once in her lifetime, Gabby was speechless. Unsure of whether she was in shock or sheer amazement, her bold eyes grew wider and open!

There were teal ones, gold ones, purple ones, coral ones, each scale glistened from the sunbeams that pried through the window. She wiggled her tail up and down and back and forth allowing the seaweed-colored ends to brush against the carpet.

"I'm...the mermaid?" Gabby tasted the words as they left her lips. "I'm the mermaid!!! How cool is this!?"

"Cool?" Cat said, puzzled. "Not only is there a mermaid on my bedroom floor, but the mermaid just so happens to be my cousin that has some major ex-plaining to do!"

Gabby was lost in her thoughts and she was content with not being found. A real-life mermaid. *Oh, all the places I could be swimming through the endless sea.*

"I could dive underwater and never lose my breath. I could talk to the flounders and touch the coral reefs. I could race against the dolphins and maybe even marry a prince," Gabby gleefully boasted.

"Gabby! This isn't some fairytale movie. Savannah, our non-mermaid baby-sitter, is downstairs waiting on us! Our parents are due back this evening! They are going to completely flip out," Cat rumbled pacing back and forth across the room.

"It must've been the potion," Gabby said. "Last night I couldn't fall asleep, so I went downstairs to re-make the potion and to see what went wrong! It just smelled so good, I thought it would be okay to try a little."

Cat could not believe what she was hearing. In a perfect world, having a magical mermaid cousin would be extraordinary. This wasn't a perfect world though!

The parentals wanted everything to

be in order just like it was when they left. That includes Gabby with feet and not a long, sparkly fin!

"Girls! Is everything okay?" Savannah yelled up from the base of the stairs.

"Uhh, yes! Coming!" Cat yelled back. Coming!? How could they be coming when Gabby couldn't even walk!

"You have to go downstairs, Cat," Gabby began. "Just tell her that I have a bit of a tummy ache. Nothing too serious, but I'd just like to rest up a bit more."

Once again, Cat was cast in a plot that only made sense in Gabby's mind. She went from being a supporting character to the main act. It was a role that she didn't even audition for.

"Fine! I'm going to go downstairs and bring breakfast up," Cat said. "Don't move!"

"Umm...I don't think I'll have a problem with that, Cat."

Cat stomped off and headed downstairs. Savannah had already set the table and was portioning the food on the plates.

"Sav, would you be totally mad if Gabby and I had breakfast in my room this morning?"

"You know what your mom says about having food upstairs, Cat."

"I know. I know. It's just that Gabby didn't sleep too well last night so she's still upstairs resting up. She's completely fine, but I just thought breakfast in bed would get her up and going," Cat smiled nervously.

She could feel a bead of sweat roll down the side of her face.

"Is it me or is it hot in here?" Cat asked, fanning herself playfully.

"It's a little warm," Savannah said. "And okay, just this one time. Make sure to leave no evidence of food anywhere. Tell Gabby that I'll be up shortly to check on her--"

"No!" Cat blurted out. "I mean, no rush at all!"

Cat grabbed the two plates and headed upstairs to her room. She opened the door to see nothing... nobody! *Don't tell me she drank an invisible ghost potion too!*

Splish. Splash. Splash. Splish. Cat walked towards the bathroom and slowly pushed the door open.

"Look at me!" Gabby snickered! "I'm the Queen of the Sea".

Gabby swayed her tail in the bathwater in a fluid sweeping motion.

"Gabby, we have to get you back to normal, now!" Cat demanded.

"Can we at least eat breakfast first?" Gabby asked. "No time for that! Out of the tub so that we can find a reversal for this potion," Cat said as she reached into the bathtub and tugged on the drain stopper.

Gabby sighed. "I guess Mermaid for the Day would be too much to ask for."

"At this point, Mermaid for the Minute will just have to do," Cat replied.

Cat helped pull Gabby gently from the garden tub.

"Do mermaids need towels?" Cat asked. The girls looked at each other and giggled.

"Face it, Cat! Having a mermaid cousin is cool and you know it."

"Having you as my cousin is cool, period! That will always be just good enough for me."

Gabby smiled, placing her little, bronzed hand over her heart.

"Now, let's get to work," said Cat.

"Let's do this!"

CHAPTER SEVEN

"It says here that to reverse the spell, the Mermaid Mystery potion has to be taken as the sunsets. Before drinking the mixture you must say: A beauty to be. A mermaid from the sea. Magic in my hand. Send me back to land," Cat read on the tablet screen.

"What time is sunset?" Gabby questioned.

"Nowadays around 7 in the evening," Cat estimated. "That's going to take forever."

The only things the girls could do was allow time to pass and keep Savannah busy downstairs. Cat had never appreciated the squeaky, creaky stairs until now. It was the perfect signal when someone was coming.

Cat grabbed the hunter green color pencil from her design kit. She had been practicing weaving and textures so Gabby had been the perfect muse for her sketch. She also was a great distraction to just how anxious Cat was, yet tried her best to hide.

"I just hope that this works," Cat mumbled.

"If not, I guess you're stuck with me like this," Gabby joked.

"Too soon, Gabby!" said Cat. "This has to work."

"Girls! We're home!"

Gabby and Cat gasped! If the walls could talk, they'd scream BUSTED!

"How is this possible?!" Cat asked, shuffling in her seat.

"How isn't it possible," Gabby replied. "Knowing your mom, she probably couldn't wait to get back here today!"

"Quick! Get under the covers!," Cat said, helping Gabby into the bed. "The sun should be setting soon. I'll go down and attempt to make it to my 8th birthday!"

Cat could just melt, but that wouldn't solve the fact that her mermaid cousin was upstairs.

Cat didn't understand how Gabby was so calm right now. Maybe it's a mermaid thing! Meanwhile,Cat tried to get the trembling of her hands under control as she turned the knob of her bedroom door.

Praying her way down the stairs she paused at the bottom step. It was like entering into a cold, dark courtroom and their parents were both the judge and the jury!

Quick! What would Gabby do? She'd be brave and act normal. She'd say, "Cat, you got this!".

"I got this," Cat said under her breath.

"Mom!" Cat said running towards her mother.

She met her with open arms and swung Cat around like a round of Ring Around the Rosie!

"Aww, Cat! You don't know how much I missed you," Mom said, her face lit up in excitement!

"I missed you so much more, Mom," Cat replied.

"The girls were wonderful Mrs. Turner," Savannah assured. "They were so helpful and surprisingly quiet and glued to the hip."

"Speaking of being glued to the hip," Gabby's mom began, "where is mine?"

Quick! What would Gabby do? Maybe, tell the truth, the whole truth, and nothing but the truth? Who am I kidding!

"Umm...she's packing up the rest of her things," Cat said, stumbling over her words. "She should be down shortly."

"Well, I'll just go up and make sure that she isn't forgetting anything," Gabby's mom said heading toward the stairs

"I wouldn't do that if I were you," Cat called out.

"Why not? We still have a long drive home and knowing Gabby she'd have me make a u-turn because she forgot a blouse or toy she claims she can't live without."

"Well, my room's not clean," Cat said nervously.

"Excuse me?," Mom said.

Boom! Clack! The floor above them let out a rumble!

"Gabby? Is that you!" Gabby's mom called out.

Mom and Sav rushed up the stairs after Gabby's mom.

"Excuse me?," Mom said.

"Cat, your room was spotless when I last checked," Savannah added.

Cat could just melt, but that wouldn't solve the fact that her mermaid cousin was upstairs.

"Did I say clean," Cat chuckled. "I meant green. You know what they say: Save the Planet. Save a life!"

Savannah looked at Mom and Mom looked at me. I looked at Gabby's mom and she had yet to blink.

Who am I kidding? I'm no Gabby!

"I'm not sure what you two are up to, but I'm going upstairs," Gabby's mom declared.

Boom! Clack! The floor above them let out a rumble!

"Gabby? Is that you!" Gabby's mom called out.

Mom and Sav rushed up the stairs after Gabby's mom.

"Umm...wait!" Cat called after them!

Mom pushed open the bedroom door as Cat rushed into the room underneath her arm.

"Hey! Mom," Gabby said standing there on her own two fin...feet!? "I'm all packed up and ready to go!"

Cat stood there in amazement! *It worked, it really worked!*

"What worked?" Mom asked.

Uh-Oh. Cat was doing it again.

"Umm...it worked!" Gabby continued. "I managed to fit everything back in my suitcase just like you like it, Mom".

Gabby jumped into her mom's arms and hugged her tight as if she never planned to let go.

"Well, thanks so much again Savannah for watching the girls," Mom said, breaking the obvious daze that Cat was still in.

"Anytime, Mrs. Turner," Savannah replied as we all headed back downstairs.

Mom and Cat walked everyone to the door as Dad's headlights peeped through the downstairs window.

"Will you be available next week to watch Cat," Mom asked. "Her father and I will be attending a gala for the company."

"Of course," Savannah smiled. "You can always count on me unless I'm somewhere traveling the sea".

Gabby and Cat gazed at each other.

"Our babysitter is a mermaid," Gabby whispered, tugging on Cat's arm.

"That's one Mermaid Mystery you'll be handling on your own," Cat said, waving bye to Savannah.

"But we're the perfect team," Gabby said, batting her eyes.

"Don't even try it," Cat replied, looking away.

"See you next time, Cat".

"See you next time, Gab".

As insane as the weekend had been, all Cat could do is smile.

What would Gabby do? She'd do it all and that is why she loved her…

THE END

ABOUT THE AUTHOR

Vicki D. Turner grew up in the small city of Franklin, KY. A graduate of Western Kentucky University & University of Tennessee, she practiced as a clinical Registered Dental Hygienist for over 15 years, taught Clinical Dental Hygiene and was a Professional Educator.

She is currently a Territory Account Executive for Procter & Gamble. Because of her seven year-old daughter□s passion for reading and imagination, she has found the love of writing and creating stories for children and youth.